11/00
04/03   13 8/09

TOAD

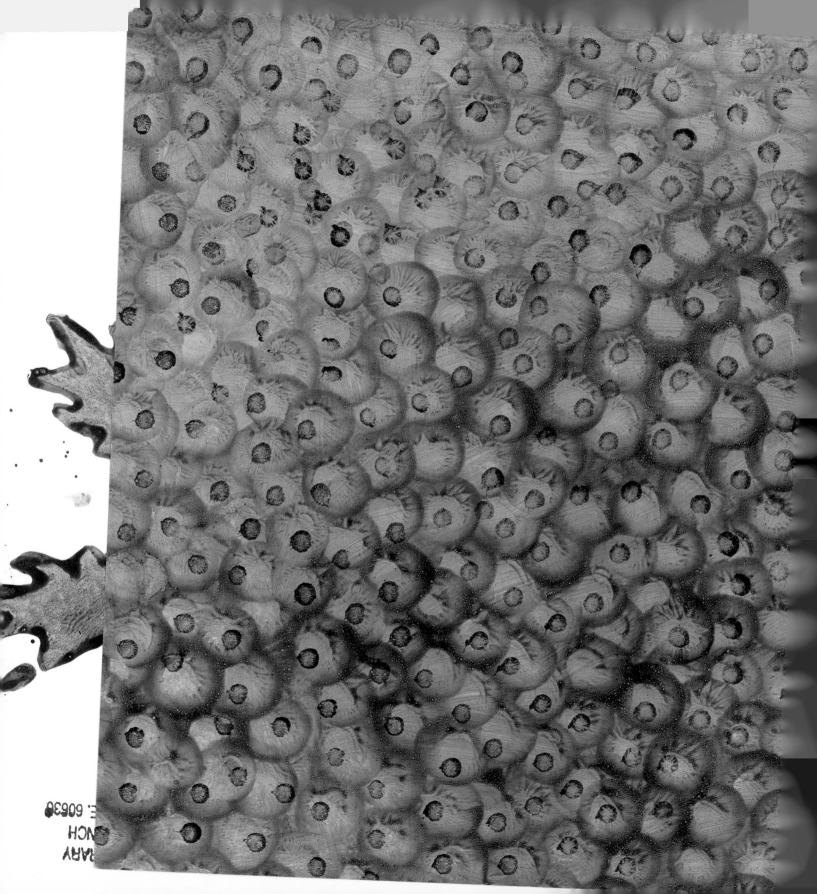

This is the tale of a toad.

A muddy toad, a mucky toad,
a clammy, sticky, gooey toad,

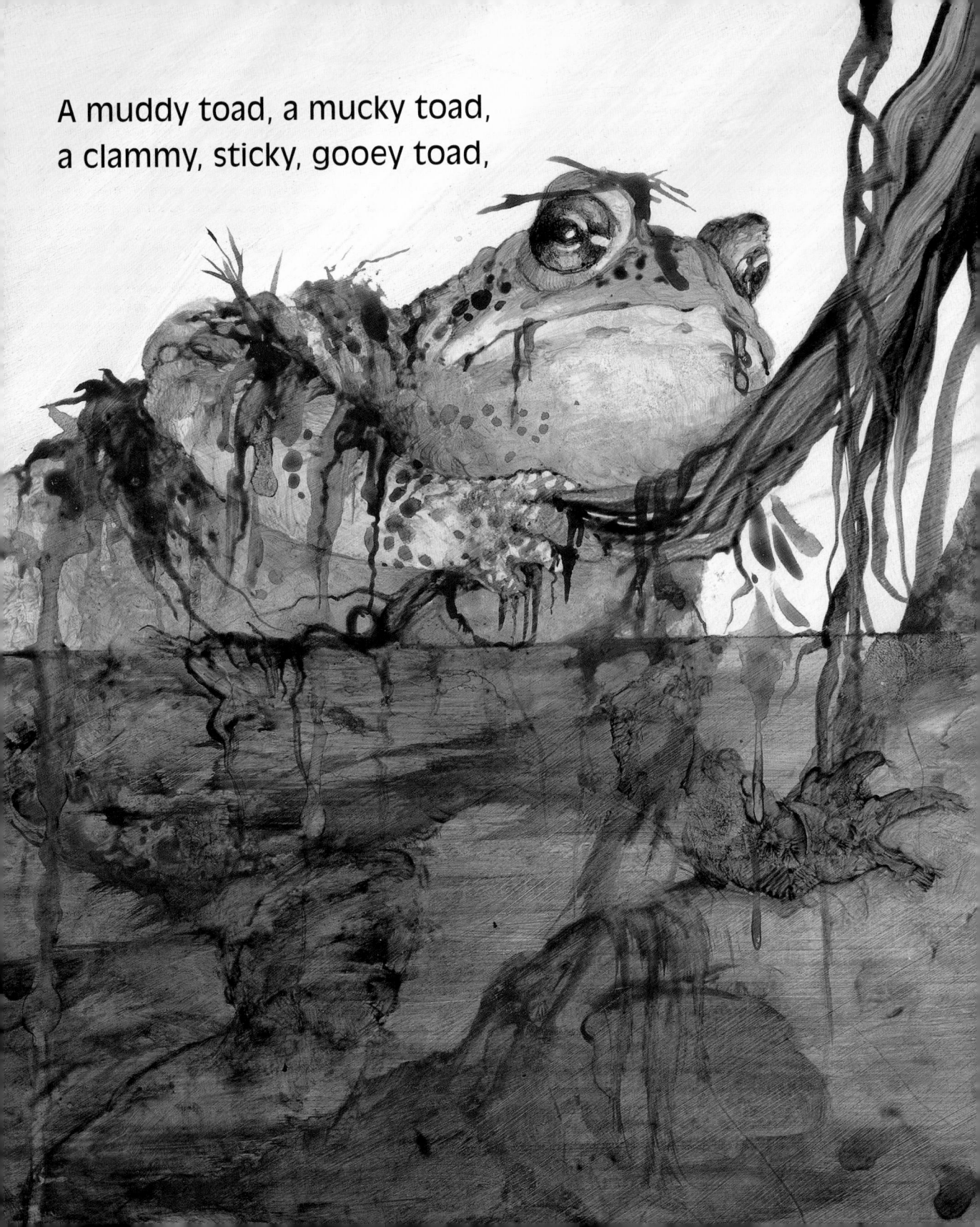

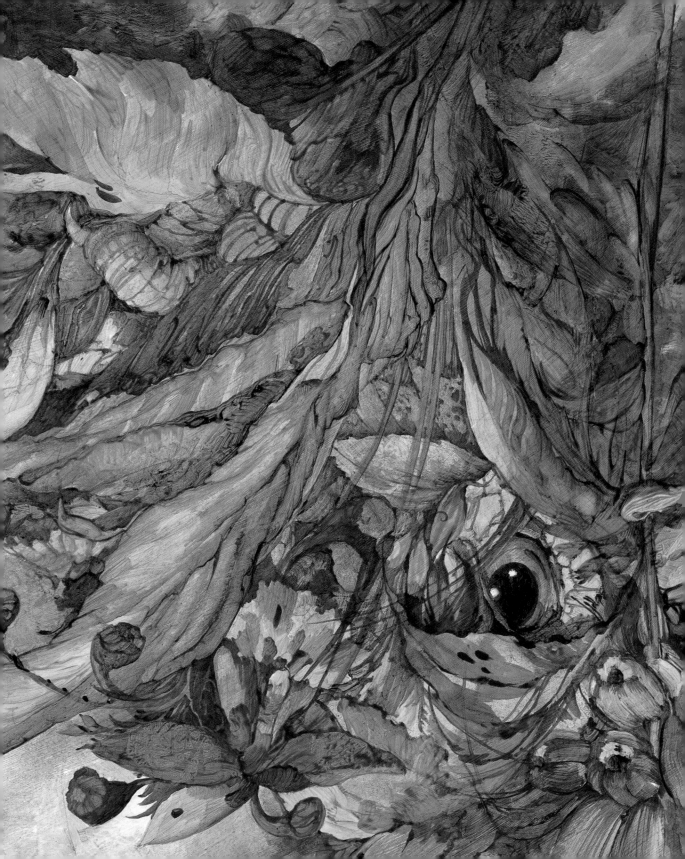

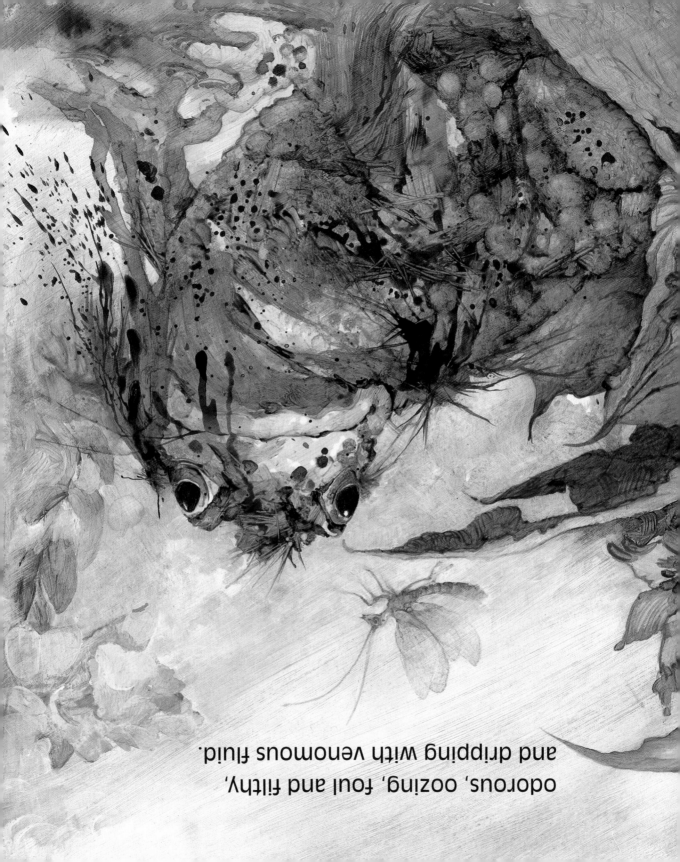

odorous, oozing, foul and filthy,
and dripping with venomous fluid.

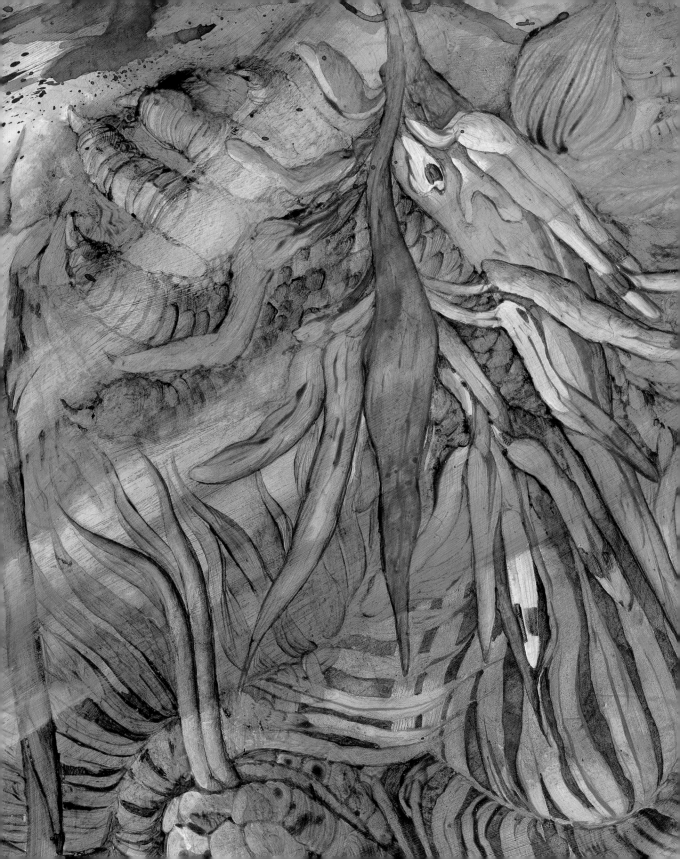

Toad's covered in warts and lumps
and bumps, with stains and
spots and speckled humps.

He's nasty, septic, toxic, and bitter,
and he leaves a slimy trail.

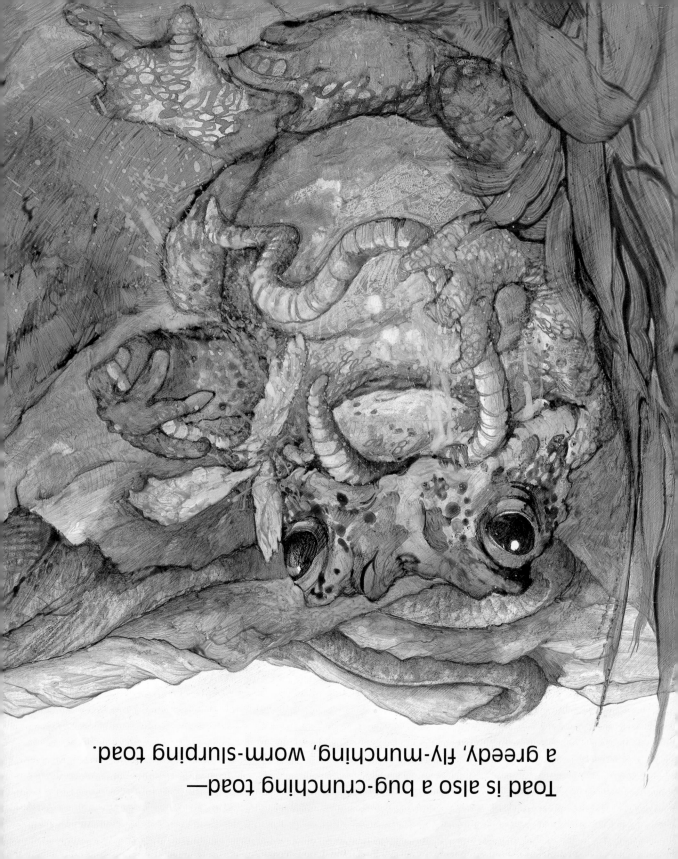

Toad is also a bug-crunching toad—
a greedy, fly-munching, worm-slurping toad.

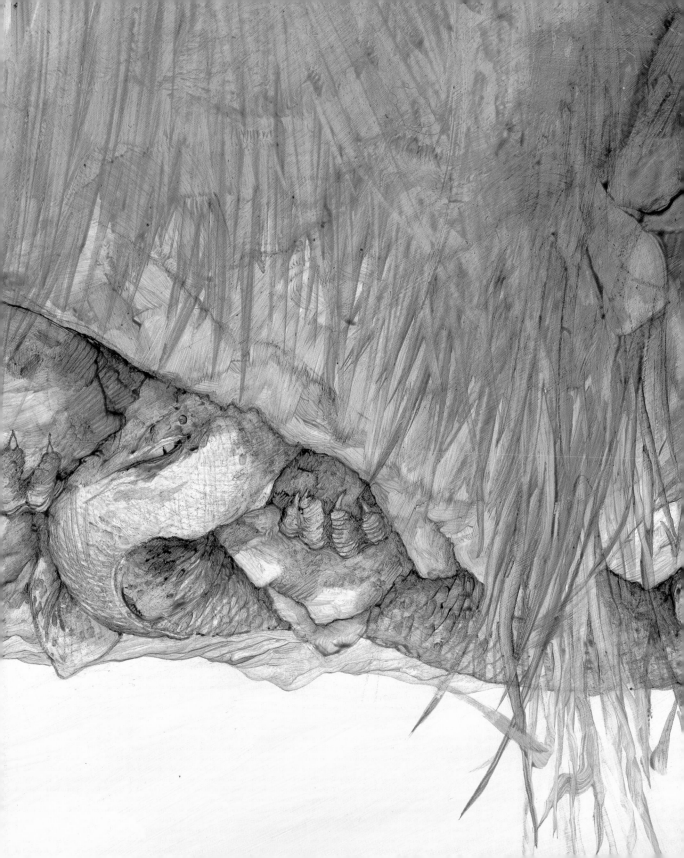

He is clumsy and careless, sluggish and slow,

and he can't even see very well.
So, winking and blinking,
he waddles and stumbles,
trudges and trundles

straight into the jaws of a monster!

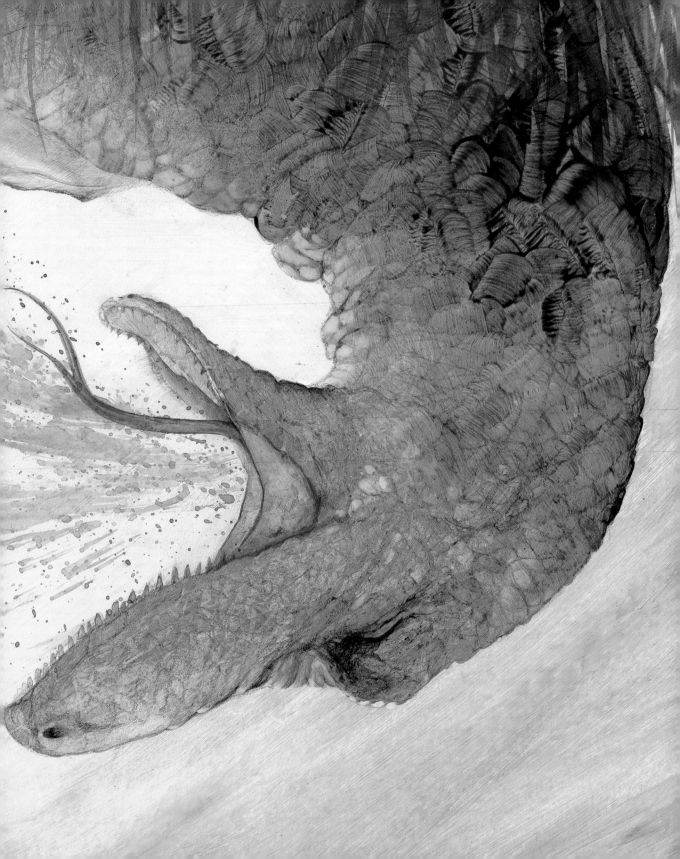

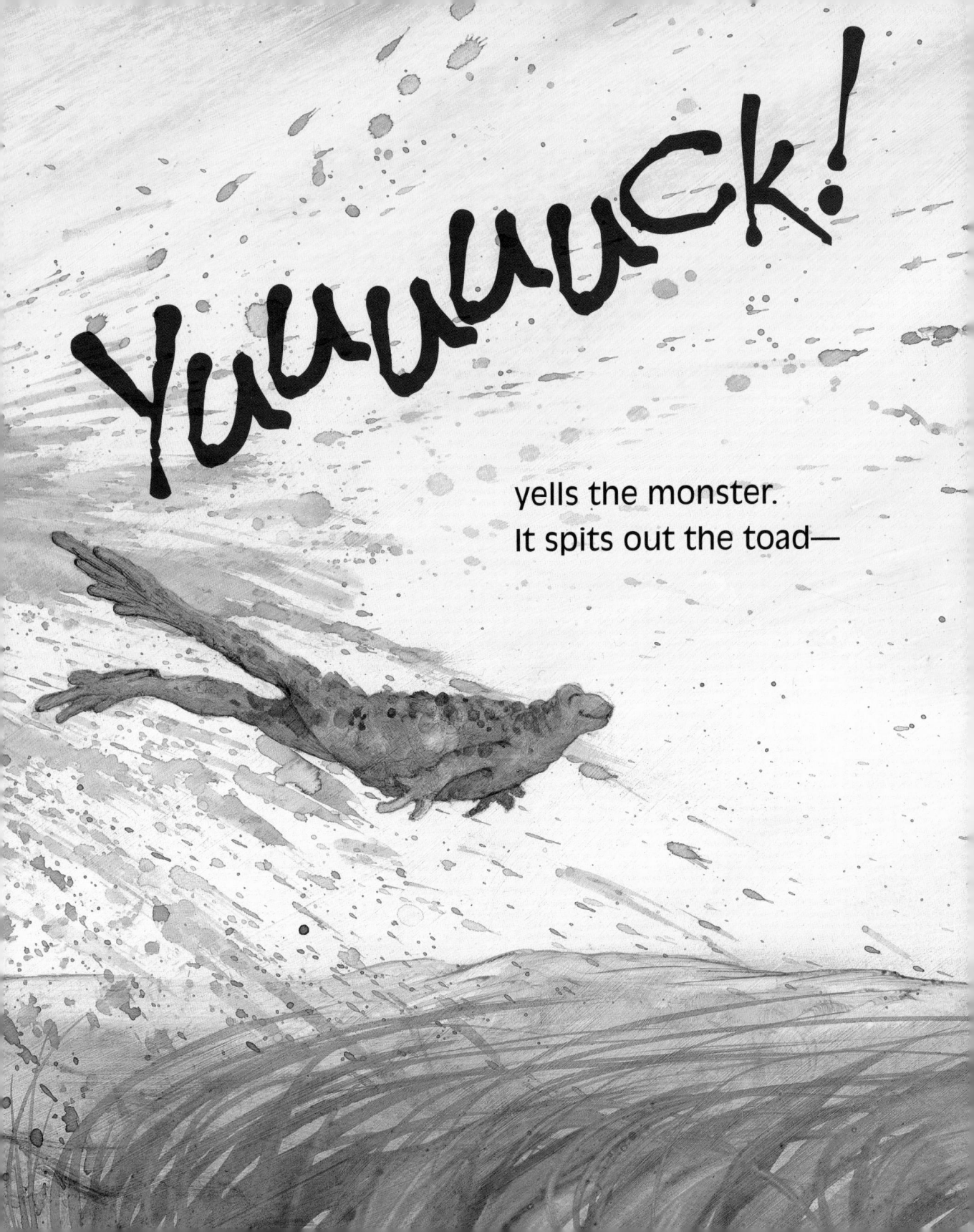

Yuuuuuck!

yells the monster.
It spits out the toad—

the happy toad, the safe toad,
the carefree and self-confident toad,

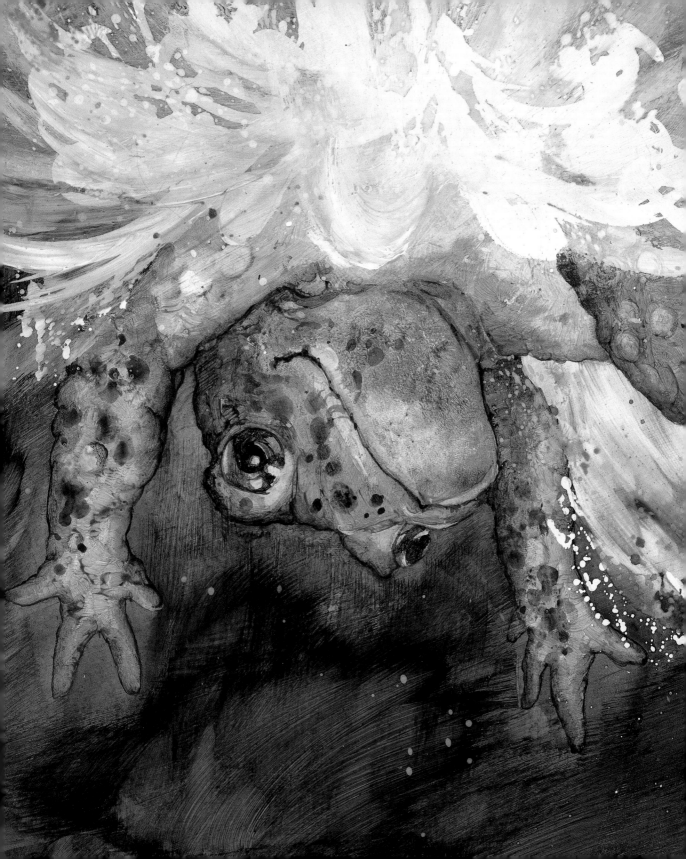

the toad with a monstrous smile.

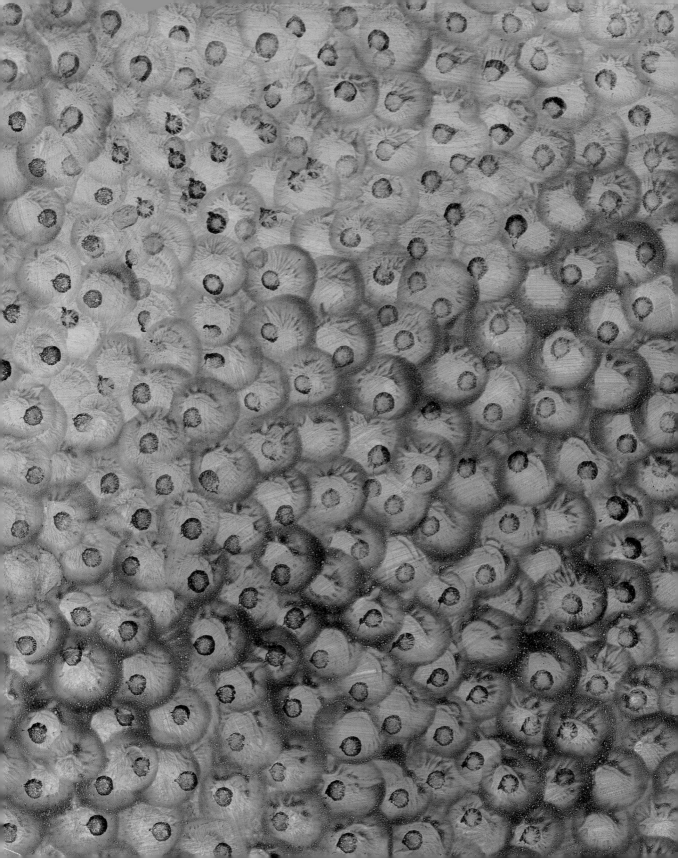